EGMONT

We bring stories to life

First published in Great Britain in 2008 by Dean,
an imprint of Egmont UK Limited
239 Kensington High Street, London W8 6SA

HiT entertainment

ISBN 978 0 6035 6258 7
5 7 9 10 8 6
Printed in Singapore

Toby had a Little Lamb

The Thomas TV Series

DEAN

It was winter on the Island of Sodor. The hills and fields were covered in snow.

Toby and Henrietta were working hard on their branchline. They were very cold.

"This isn't much fun," said Toby. "I can't wait to get into my nice, dry shed."

But suddenly Toby's Driver applied the brakes! Farmer McColl was standing by the side of the line, waving a big red flag.

"Please help me!" cried Farmer McColl. "My phone lines are down, all the roads are blocked, and my sheep have just started lambing! They're trapped on the hillside, cut off by the snow!"

"How can we help?" Toby asked at once.

"I need a vet as quickly as possible!" said the worried farmer.

"We'll stop at the next signalbox," said Toby's Driver. "I'll phone the vet from there."

Toby raced to the signalbox. The Driver
called ahead to Callan Station and explained the
problem. When they arrived at the station, The Fat
Controller was already waiting with the vet.

"I'll send Duck to the farm right away,"
said The Fat Controller. "This is a job
for an engine with a snowplough."

Duck battled bravely along the track. But too much snow had fallen, and the line ahead was blocked. "We can't carry on," said Duck's Driver, grimly. "We'll have to go back."

Toby was very surprised to see Duck return to the station.

"I tried my hardest," puffed Duck, "but even my snowplough can't get through."

The Fat Controller was very worried.

Then Toby had an idea.

"We could use my old branchline, Sir! I know that line like the back of my buffers. It's our only chance to help the baby lambs!" said Toby.

The Fat Controller agreed and the vet climbed aboard Henrietta.

Toby struggled along the old branchline.

The blizzard was very bad and Toby's Driver was worried.

"Perhaps we should go back," said his Driver.

"I can do it!" called Toby. "As long as these lines hold!"

But Toby had forgotten about the rickety old bridge. As he started to cross it, he could feel his wheels wobbling. His Driver tried to keep him steady.

"I've got to reach the other side of this bridge!" gasped Toby. "Those lambs need me!"

At last Toby reached Farmer McColl.

He was waiting in the cold, and he smiled when he saw Toby's headlamp shining through the snowstorm.

"You made it!" cried Farmer McColl. "What a brave engine you are!"

Farmer McColl took the vet to see the lambs.

Toby waited for them to come back, hoping the lambs would be all right. At last he saw Farmer McColl in the distance.

"The baby lambs are safe and sound, Toby!" called Farmer McColl. "But we need a place to keep the little ones warm and dry."

Toby smiled. "Henrietta has plenty of room," he said.

So Farmer McColl and the vet brought the little lambs to shelter inside Henrietta.

Toby and Henrietta stayed at the farm for several days, just to make sure that the lambs were all right. At last the blizzard ended, and the sun shone down.

Farmer McColl was very grateful.

"Thank you, Toby," he said. "We couldn't have done it without you!"

"No. Thank *you*!" said Toby. "There's nothing I like better than helping out a friend in need!"